D

For Luke and Lydia, with love – AM

First published in 2001
This edition re-issued in 2011

Text copyright © Anthony Masters 2001
Illustrations copyright © Stephen Player 2001

Wayland
338 Euston Road
London NW1 3BH

Wayland Australia
Level 17/207 Kent Street
Sydney, NSW 2000

British Library Cataloguing in Publication Data available

ISBN 978 0 7502 6559 1

Printed in China

Wayland is a division of Hachette Children's Books,
an Hachette UK company

ANTHONY MASTERS

Deadly Dodgem

Illustrated by Stephen Player

WAYLAND

Chapter One

Jack sat up in bed and glanced at his watch.
It was just after midnight. Lights were
sweeping his room.

Jack ran to the window. The dodgem track at the end of the pier was floodlit and there was the sound of bumping and crashing. He gazed out in disbelief, unable to work out what was happening.

Jack's parents were fast asleep. They owned the dodgem track and had both gone to bed so tired that he didn't want to wake them.

Creeping downstairs and tiptoeing across the kitchen, Jack gently slipped the latch and began to hurry along the sea front towards the pier.

Suddenly the spotlights on the track switched off and the bumping and crashing sounds stopped.

The silence was very deep.

Jack was sweating in the warm August night. He stared at the darkened pier. The power must have been left on. But then who had switched it off again? If someone had got into the control room, they might still be around. Jack wondered if he should go home again, wake his parents and get them to phone the police.

He turned round and began to walk back towards the house. This was someone else's problem. Not his.

Then he remembered how exhausted his parents were. Maybe he should try and solve the problem for them, on his own.

Determined not to panic, Jack turned back. If he saw anyone on the pier, he'd run for it. He'd always been fast on his feet.

The sea front was completely deserted. Jack climbed over the gates of the pier and dropped down on the other side. Nothing stirred. Dark water slopped and sighed under the slats beneath his feet. There was a strong smell of rotting seaweed.

Suddenly the spotlights came on again and Jack heard the dodgems start up. He froze. What was making the electricity cut in and out like that?

Jack's heart was beating painfully when he reached the track, expecting to see a gang riding the cars. But to his amazement the dodgems were completely empty. Even stranger, the other dodgems had surrounded a single car. Number Six.

Suddenly Number Six seemed to go crazy, its steering wheel twisting and turning, ramming the other cars until they were spinning in circles. It was as if the dodgems had minds of their own...

Jack raced over to the control room, but it was locked. He paused for a moment, unsure of what to do. He needed to see if the lever was down – which would mean that the power was on. He jumped up, hung on to the edge of the window-sill and looked inside.

The lever was up. The power wasn't on at all.

This is weird, thought Jack. How could the cars have started up with the power switched off? There was now an icy chill in the air and Jack was shivering.

He ran back on to the track and saw that Number Six was once again surrounded. But as he hesitated, the dodgems suddenly came to a halt and the spotlights went out again.

Jack was alone in the pale cold moonlight, and he could see what seemed to be a misty patch in the driver's seat of Number Six.

Then he realized that the mist had a shape. Like a figure. Jack shuddered. He couldn't believe his own eyes. He had to be mistaken.

Then the mist seemed to fade away to nothing.

Jack waited uncertainly. He could smell grease and stale popcorn and the fresh coat of paint his dad had given all the dodgems. Everything seemed quiet and calm again. Totally calm. A small breeze stirred and Jack started as an empty hamburger wrapper blew across the track.

Jack ran back down the pier and clambered over the gate. But as he jumped down on to the promenade the seam on the leg of his jeans ripped. Now he was going to be in trouble with his mum.

Chapter Two

When Jack woke the next morning he was
sure he must have been dreaming about
the battling dodgems.

He got out of bed and then saw that the
seam on the leg of his jeans had split from
top to bottom. How on earth had he
managed to rip them like that?

But then he knew what he'd done.
He hadn't been dreaming at all.

Jack felt a wave of panic. If he *hadn't* been dreaming, how could the dodgems have steered themselves? And why had Number Six gone crazy like that? Then Jack remembered that particular dodgem was new. Could Number Six have some way of setting off the others?

Jack wondered if he should tell his parents. But even if he did, he was sure they'd never believe him, unless he could prove that there was some kind of technical problem with the car.

Chapter Three

"You're winding me up, aren't you?" said Jack's best friend, Sam, when he told him what had happened. "You just had a bad dream."

"What about my jeans?"

Sam shrugged. They were standing outside the entrance to the pier. The day was hot and the beach and sea front were crowded.

"I'm telling the truth," Jack insisted. "Dad only just bought Number Six," he added.

"Really?" asked Sam, stifling a yawn.

"I'm going to give Number Six a test drive," Jack said uneasily. "I want to see if there's some kind of technical fault."

"Give us a free go then."

Jack nodded wearily. Sam was always after free rides.

The pier was packed, but because he was the son of the owners, Jack was able to get Sam a free ride and drive Number Six himself.

"I want to give that new one a whirl," Jack said to Pete, one of the attendants.

"And so you shall," said Pete with a grin. "Number Six is a real goer."

Chapter Four

Jack clambered into Number Six and put on the safety belt. Suddenly he felt angry with Sam. Very angry.

Jack saw Sam climb into Number Four. He'd get Sam for not believing what had happened last night.

As Number Six began to move, Jack's anger mounted.

Head-on bumping wasn't allowed and there were notices pinned up all round the track. But Jack didn't pay any attention. He was furious. He drove at Sam, crashing head-on, time and time again.

Sam was jerked backwards and forwards.

Jack laughed nastily. He was enjoying giving Sam a hard time.

Then Sam hit himself on the steering wheel and blood poured from a cut on his chin.

The dodgems came to a halt and Jack glared up at the control room in fury.

He saw Bill, the operator, frowning down at him.

Pete strode up. "Get out!" he yelled.

Jack reluctantly did as he was told.

Sam staggered out of his dodgem, dabbing at the blood on his chin with a dirty-looking hanky.

Jack's rage vanished as quickly as it had flared up. He gazed at Sam in horror. What had he been doing? Why had he bullied his friend like that? He felt terrible.

Pete grabbed Jack's shoulder and spun him round.

"You ought to be ashamed of yourself. You know you're not allowed to bump head-on!"

"I'm sorry," Jack mumbled, trying to wrench himself out of Pete's grip, anxious to catch up with Sam and apologize.

Pete pushed Jack away. "You ought to know better."

Jack stumbled and then fell back against Number Six.

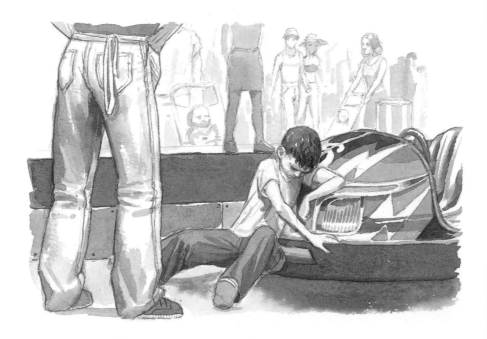

Suddenly Jack lost his temper again and kicked out wildly at the dodgem, leaving a mark on the bright new paintwork.

Now Bill was running down the control-room steps. "Get off the track!" he yelled. "I'm telling your dad about this."

As Jack ran across the track, his temper began to fade.

When he looked back he thought he could see the misty shape back in the driving seat of Number Six.

Chapter Five

"Sam... *Stop*! I'm sorry."

Jack was confused and afraid. Losing his temper like that was weird. He normally didn't have a temper to lose. It *had* to be something to do with Number Six. Jack was sure he only felt angry when he was around that dodgem.

Sam turned, still dabbing at his chin. "Push off," he snarled. He couldn't believe what Jack had done to him.

"Look, it wasn't my fault," Jack pleaded.
"Whose fault was it then?"
"That dodgem – that Number Six."
Sam gazed at his friend in amazement.

"You've got to believe me. Number Six makes me lose my temper."

Sam stared at Jack, wondering if this was another wind-up, but Jack really seemed frightened.

"What are you going to do about it then?"

"I want you to help me find out what's going on. There's something wrong with that dodgem. Something I can't explain. Dad bought Number Six at an auction in a fairground up the coast. Maybe someone there knows more about it. We could cycle over. You coming?"

There was an uneasy silence.

"I suppose," said Sam grudgingly.

Cycling in the heat was tough, but Jack didn't feel in the least bad-tempered. All he did feel was afraid that something had gone out of control. But what?

When they reached Freddy's Fabulous Funfair Jack and Sam discovered that there was no dodgem track, which seemed a bit odd.

Jack saw a girl on the candyfloss stall near the entrance and asked, "Why isn't there a dodgem track here?"

"There was, until the accident," she replied quietly.

Then the girl looked wary, as if she didn't want to talk to them. Jack noticed that there were tears in her eyes.

"What kind of accident?" asked Sam gently.

She shook her head.

"Listen, you've *got* to tell us what happened." Jack was feeling more and more uneasy.

The girl began to cry. "After the accident, Dad got rid of the dodgems. Most of the cars went up North, but one of them was bought locally."

"Can you remember which one?" asked Jack, fearfully. But somehow he already knew the answer.

"Number Six," said the girl.

Just then an older boy came up, looking threatening.

"You all right, Amy?" he asked the girl, staring at Jack and Sam menacingly. Amy didn't reply, but tears were streaming down her cheeks.

"Can't you see you're upsetting her?" said the boy. "Why don't you leave her alone?"

"Is there anything else you can tell us?" asked Sam.

Amy shook her head. "Please go away. I don't want to talk about it any more."

"So do what she says," said the boy.

As they cycled home, Sam said to Jack, "What now?"

Jack shrugged. He hadn't told Sam about the misty figure he thought he'd seen in the driving seat of Number Six. But how could he? Sam would really think he'd flipped.

"I don't think Amy told us everything," said Sam.

"You bet she didn't," muttered Jack.

Chapter Six

That afternoon the dodgem track was really busy. Luckily for Jack, Bill and Pete were off duty and Dad had driven into town with Mum.

Jack headed towards the cars. "I'm going to give Number Six another try," he said to Sam, trying to build up his courage. "There's some kind of power in that dodgem, and I don't mean electrical. I've got to find out what's causing it."

"I'll come with you." Sam looked uneasy, wondering if Jack was beginning to crack up.

"Thanks." Jack walked across to the track, trying to keep calm.

"Just one go," said Mick, who was on the afternoon shift.

Jack and Sam got into Number Six and put on their safety belts.

"How do you feel?" asked Sam nervously.

"OK."

"You're not – like angry?"

But Jack didn't hear. He was staring out at the edge of the track. "Hang on. Looks like we got trouble."

A group of older boys was running towards the dodgems, shouting and yelling as they each grabbed a car.

Soon the gang began to slam their
dodgems into the other cars, frightening
some of the younger children.

Jack suddenly felt a flash of blinding rage.
"Let's get 'em," he snarled.

Sam hung on fearfully as Jack drove
Number Six at the gang's cars, taking them
head-on, making their dodgems spin out of
control. He closed his eyes as Jack swung
the car from side to side.

Suddenly, to Sam's great relief, the power
was switched off – and the dodgems drifted
to a halt.

"I'm calling the police," yelled Mick.
"I should never have let that lot on in
the first place."

Jack leapt out of Number Six and raced
after the retreating gang. He was furious.
And this time his anger didn't go away.

"Come back!" yelled Sam. "Don't get
into any more trouble."

But Jack wasn't listening.

Chapter Seven

Sam began to run across the track after
Jack, but bumped straight into someone.
It was Amy.

"I've come to tell you something."

"What is it?" snapped Sam.

"I should have told you before, but I was too upset. My brother, Steve, had this temper. He was always getting angry. One day he took on this gang who were smashing up the track. Steve fell over and hit his head on Number Six. He got killed."

Amy gave a sob, but Sam was already on the move. He had seen Jack running back over the track, pursued by a couple of members of the gang.

"We're going to get you," yelled one of the older boys.

"Try me," snarled Jack, his fists clenched. He was standing very close to Number Six now. Too close.

"He doesn't stand a chance," gasped Amy as the gang moved nearer.

"Jack's never been much of a fighter," muttered Sam.

"Steve was," said Amy as she moved between Jack and the gang. "I know you!" she yelled at one of the thugs. "You had a go at my brother, didn't you?"

"Look out!" yelled Sam, pushing Amy and Jack to one side.

Number Six was starting to move – all on its own. The dodgem's steering wheel was turning wildly. Number Six was heading straight for the two members of the gang.

They stared at Number Six horrified, as
a puff of mist appeared in the driver's seat.
Slowly it turned into the faint outline of
a boy – someone they recognized.

Sam glanced at Amy and knew that she had seen her brother, too.

Number Six began to chase the two boys around the track, herding them up like sheep and then allowing them to scatter again. Several times they almost managed to escape, but just at the last minute the dodgem blocked their path. They didn't look at all frightening now. They looked terrified.

"Let them go now, Steve," pleaded Amy at last. "They'll remember this as long as they live."

Number Six screamed to a rattling halt.

Shaking with fear, the two boys stared at it. Then, before they could be attacked again, they fled.

"Look!" Amy grabbed Jack's arm and pointed as the misty shape rose out of Number Six, drifting into the air, getting fainter all the time.

Amy, Jack and Sam watched the last strand of mist disappear.

Half-an-hour later, Jack drove Number Six around the track, watched by Sam and Amy. When the dodgem came to a halt they ran over to him.

"Looks like Number Six is back to normal," Jack said. "Want a ride, Amy?"

As she climbed in, she whispered, "Steve's gone."

And taken his temper with him, thought Jack in relief.

DARE TO BE SCARED!

Are you brave enough to try more titles in the Tremors series? They're guaranteed to chill your spine...

The Haunted Mine by Jan Dean
When Dodge and Berto see six ghostly shapes rise out of the smoke at the old mine, they run away as fast as they can. But now the ghosts know where they live. Who are they? And what do they want?

Beware the Wicked Web by Anthony Masters
In the dead of night, Rob and Sam explore the forbidden attic at the top of their new home. When they find a sprawling, sticky web, with a giant egg at its centre, they are scared – but not nearly as scared as when they discover that the egg is just about to hatch...

The Empty Grave by Rebecca Lisle
When Jay visits her cousin at Gulliver House, strange things start to happen. Who is the mysterious child that cries in the night? And what is behind the sealed door? Jay and Freddie must discover the truth before it's too late...

All these books and many more can be purchased from your local bookseller. For more information about Tremors, write to: The Sales Department, Hachette Children's Books, 338 Euston Road, London NW1 3BH.